D0811170

© Oyster Books Ltd. 1991
First published 1991 by Blackie & Son Ltd.,
7 Leicester Place, London WC2H 7BP

Printed and bound in Singapore

CIP data available

MY FAIRY TALE LIBRARY
(8 titles in slipcase)
ISBN 0 216 93117 7

*Cinderella*
*Goldilocks and the Three Bears*
*Hansel and Gretel*
*Jack and the Beanstalk*
*Little Red Riding Hood*
*Puss in Boots*
*Snow White and the Seven Dwarfs*
*The Sleeping Beauty*

Text adapted from the original fairy tales
and retold by Tim and Jenny Wood

Design by Pinpoint Design Ltd

# GOLDILOCKS
## AND THE
# THREE BEARS

BLACKIE

Once upon a time there were three
bears who lived in a cottage in
a forest. There was Father Bear
who was very big and had a deep,
growly voice. There was Mother
Bear who was medium-sized and
had a soft, gentle voice. And there
was Baby Bear who was very
small indeed and had a tiny,
squeaky voice.

The Three Bears each had their very own chair,

their very own bed,

their very own porridge bowl and their very own spoon.

One fine morning Mother Bear made a huge pot of hot porridge for her family, just as she did every day. There was a great big bowl of porridge for Father Bear, a medium-sized bowl for Mother Bear, and a tiny little bowl for Baby Bear.

But when the Three Bears tasted their porridge, they found it was much too hot.

'Ouch!' cried Baby Bear in his tiny, squeaky voice. 'I've burnt my mouth!'

'Let's go for a walk in the forest while our porridge cools down,' suggested Mother Bear. And off they went.

No sooner had
the Three
Bears left
their cottage
than a little girl
stopped at the
front gate. Her
name was Goldilocks, because her
hair was a mass of golden curls.
She lived right on the other side
of the forest. She had been
walking for a long time and was
very hungry and tired. The front
door of the cottage was open, so
Goldilocks peeped inside.

'Is anyone there?' she cried.

There was no answer.

Goldilocks tiptoed into the kitchen. When she saw the three bowls of porridge, Goldilocks felt hungrier than ever.

She picked up the great big spoon and tasted the porridge in Father Bear's great big bowl. It was much too hot. Then she picked up the medium-sized spoon and tasted the porridge in Mother Bear's medium-sized bowl, but that was much too cold. Then she picked up the tiny little spoon and tasted the porridge in Baby Bear's tiny little bowl. It tasted just right, and Goldilocks ate it all up!

'I feel quite tired now,' said Goldilocks to herself. 'I think I'll just sit down and have a rest.'

First Goldilocks sat down in Father Bear's great big chair, but it was much too hard.

Then she sat down in Mother Bear's medium-sized chair, but it was much too soft.

Then she tried Baby Bear's tiny little chair. It felt just right, but when Goldilocks sat right down on it . . . crack!, the chair broke into pieces. Goldilocks was very upset, but there was nothing she could do to mend the chair.

Goldilocks still felt tired so she went into the bedroom. There she saw a great big bed, a medium-sized bed and a tiny little bed.

'Perhaps I could have a little sleep,' she yawned.

So Goldilocks climbed up on to Father Bear's great big bed. But

when she lay down she found it was much too hard. So she climbed down and tried Mother Bear's medium-sized bed.

But that was much too soft. Then she lay down on Baby Bear's tiny little bed. It was just right!
Goldilocks was soon fast asleep.

Not long afterwards, the Three Bears returned from their walk. The fresh air had made them hungry. As they came into the kitchen, they stared in surprise at the bowls of porridge on the table.

'Who's been eating my porridge?' roared Father Bear in his deep, growly voice.

'Who's been eating my porridge?' cried Mother Bear in her soft, gentle voice.

'Who's been eating my porridge – and eaten it all up?' wailed Baby Bear in his tiny, squeaky voice.

Then Father Bear looked at his great big chair. 'Who's been sitting in my chair?' he roared in his deep, growly voice.

Mother Bear looked at her medium-sized chair.

'Who's been sitting in my chair?' she cried in her soft, gentle voice.

Baby Bear looked at his tiny, little chair.

'Who's been sitting in my chair – and broken it into pieces?' he wailed in his tiny, squeaky voice.

'Someone's been in our house!' roared Father Bear. 'Let's search the other rooms and see if they're still here!'

The Three Bears tiptoed round the house, looking in all the rooms, but there was no sign of anyone. Then they went into their bedroom.

Father Bear looked at his great big bed. The cover was all crumpled.

'Who's been sleeping in my bed?' he roared in his deep, growly voice.

Mother Bear looked at her medium-sized bed. The bedclothes had been turned back.

'Who's been sleeping in my bed?' she cried in her soft, gentle voice.

Baby Bear looked at his tiny little bed. 'Look!' he squeaked in his tiny, squeaky voice. 'Somebody's been sleeping in my bed, and they're still there now!'

Goldilocks woke with a start. When she saw the Three Bears standing round the bed, she felt very frightened.

Goldilocks jumped out of bed
and ran out of the house. She
raced through the forest as fast
as her legs could carry her, and
didn't stop until she reached her
own little house. She vowed never
to go into the forest again.

As for the Three Bears, Father Bear quickly mended Baby Bear's tiny little chair and Mother Bear soon had another pot of porridge bubbling on the stove.